AF176556

Story 'No Mandate for Christmas'
Nr. III of the serie „Christmas Scenes"
2021©Copyright: Hiam Mondini
Edit: Nicholas Modlin
Cover: Angelina Brianna Mondini
Printed and published: BoD – Books on Demand, Norderstedt
ISBN: 9783755760092

***

No Mandate
for Christmas

***

Christmas Scene III

by

Hiam Mondini

Inspired by the life in the canton of
Zug / Switzerland in 2021

Preface

When I returned to my home canton this summer after three years in Chicago, I noticed how quickly time had been turning in my absence. How much growth there was and what enormous, classified differences there are now.

In the city there are so many new families from all over the world as well as Swiss families who are increasingly pursuing inner tranquility in the nature that surrounds us.

I am reminded of these things each time I listen to the stories my children bring home after visiting the families of our city. Stories like these keep them thoughtfulness and help them to see how different every little world can be.

With this in mind, I sincerely wish everyone a Merry Christmas with family, friends and plenty of time to recognize and appreciate the essential things in life.

December 20, 2021

„Food is ready!"

Busy and focused, the sturdy, small woman puts a steaming bowl on the set table. She looks around and lifts a finger.

„Bent, could you please get another bottle of apple juice from the cellar? And Alessia, take a quick look at the chickens to see if there are any eggs left. But make it quick or the soup will get cold." She wipes her hand on her apron while looking at the table with satisfaction.

„Bread." The word flits over her lips and, as if her thought had been read, a little boy lifts a loaf of bread to her.

„You are a clairvoyant, Timon. Thank you, my big boy. Have you washed your hands yet?" She takes the little one's warm hands in hers and raises an eyebrow.

„Well, I'll turn a blind eye, but you won't get a medal for this. And today we're going to cut your nails so there's no more room for the dirt to hide underneath." She gives him his hands back and winks happily.

„Who is hiding?" Bent emerges into the rustic dining room with a corked bottle and puts the fresh apple juice on the wooden table.

„The dirt under my nails! Show me yours!" Timon tries to grab his older brother's hand, but they retreat into Bent's pockets before they can be reached.

„Nothing to see here, buddy. Sit down, you dwarf!" As he sais this, he sits down on a wooden chair at the table, still with both hands tucked away.

„Because you eat them all up, you pig!" Alessia stands under the door frame and holds two eggs in each hand. She sticks out her tongue at her brother and carefully brings the eggs to the kitchen counter and places them in a small basket. She looks proudly at the various hues of beige, brown, white, and green coloring each egg and nods approvingly.

„If you stare at those eggs for a long enough time, you'll be ducking like a real chicken yourself. Just wait, you will soon grow feathers of your own and be able to lay eggs too. Let's make a bet what color yours will be! I'll go for pink." Bent laughs out loud and considers breaking off a piece of bread when his mother comes through the door next to Alessia.

„Stop the nasty quarreling now! Your father is coming home

soon, and I am sure he is looking forward to a pleasant evening. Thanks for the eggs, Alessia. They look great, don't they? Please wash your hands, dear. And you wait with the bread, young man!" She raises an eyebrow at her eldest son as she takes her seat at the table.

At that very moment, sounds of the front door unlatching and heavy shoes falling on wooden flooring echoe through the hallway.

„Helloooo rascals!" The deep voice fills the house and a small, strong man emerges into the dining room, his eyes sparkling at the sight of his loved ones. He claps his hands, rubs them together and walks towards the table.

„Hmmmm, it smells wonderful in here and looks so inviting, Mom! What a lucky guy I am!" He walks around the table, places his big, warm hands on his wife's shoulders and kisses her on the head.

„Thank you, my love!"

„You're very welcome. Sit down, the children are hungry."

Maria nods her husband towards the opposite side of the table and begins to scoop hot soup into the bowls.

After a few minutes of slurping and lip-smacking go by, when Timon begins to shift around uneasily on his chair.

„Dad, why aren't we praying?" Timon stuffs the bread that has just been dipped in the soup into his mouth and chews loudly.

„God wouldn't hear our prayer with you smacking your lips so loudly. Close your mouth, please!"

Bent shakes his head in and treats himself to a full spoonful of soup.

The father smiles and replies softly, „You can pray any time, Timon. And if it means something to you, we will join you together at the table. I like to pray by saying thank you to those who matter to me. I am thankful for the wonderful food that your mother prepares for us so often and I am thankful for having each of you kids in my life every day." He takes a piece of bread, tears it in half and looks lovingly at his youngest child.

„What do you say thank you for, Mom?" The big, googly eyes of the smallest in the family wander from father to mother.

Maria puts her spoon back in the bowl and takes a deep breath. She looks around the table and replies: „I'm grateful every day for our health and the wealth we have."

At these words, Alessia makes a loud choking, disparaging noise.

„Alessia, do you disagree with what I just said?" Maria brings a spoon to her mouth and looks at her daughter questioningly.

„Wealth? Us rich?" The teenage girl looks around the simple room and heretically raises her eyebrows. „I'll tell you who is rich. Dina's family, they are really rich! Their mother AND father drive a car and they all have modern bicycles too. Imagine, Dina even has her own TV in her room. But while I'm at it, they go on such amazing trips every weekend, just Dina and her mom. They spend weekends in Paris eating croissants for breakfast by the Eiffel Tower. I'm the one who grew

17

up here in Switzerland, but Dina still has me beat! She has been to every mountain in the country. Really, EVERY SINGLE ONE. One gondola ride here, one chairlift there. It is a miracle that they haven't landed a helicopter on the Matterhorn yet; they have already flown around it. I saw the photos! She was even allowed to sit next to the pilot. Awesome, don't you think? That's being rich, Mom!" The passionate girl throws both hands in the air as if she had just made an enormous breakthrough in a court hearing.

The silence at the table hangs heavy for a moment as all eyes are on Alessia. Then, without speaking, one by one the family members turn back to their bowls and continue to slurp their dinner.

December 21, 2021

Maria carefully takes one box after the other from the shelf and places them on the table next to the cellar door. She cleverly folds the ladder up and puts it back in its designated place.

In the background, a slamming door sounds through the house quickly followed by the voice of her youngest.

„Mummy?! Maaaammmaaaa!!!!" The voice screams through the house.

„I'm in the basement, Timon!" Replies Maria. „Can you please help me carry up the Christmas boxes? Is Alessia there too?"

„Yeah, we'll be right there. Aleeeeessiiaaaaa!!!! We have to help Mom!!! In the basement!!!" The youngest of the family lets his vocal cords vibrate as he screeches loudly and steps down the wooden stairs to the cellar. The steps crunch under his stamping feet.

„Hooray, are we decorating for Christmas today? Our teacher said that this will only be done on December 24th in Switzerland. Is that right Mama? She said that in America, for example, everything has been glowing and sparkling for a long time, so much earlier than here. Have you ever been to America, Mom?" His torrent of speech is interrupted by his sister, who apparently doesn't share his cheerful mood.

„Oh man, can you shut it? My ears are about to fall off." She gives him an annoyed look and then turns to her mother. „Mom, do I always have to walk home with this chatterbox? He is so annoying. My friends don't even want to walk with me anymore because he constantly asks questions that, firstly, are none of his business and, secondly, he doesn't even wait for the answers. Really!" She narrows her gaze her eyes and crosses her arms over her chest.

„Hey, Alessia, dear, what's the matter with you?" Her mother walks up and strokes her head lovingly. „You seem like you woke up on the wrong side of the bed today? Didn't you have a good day?"

A shrug is the only answer she gets.

„Well, maybe you will be in the mood to tell me later. Come on, help me carry up these boxes. And no, Timon, we're not decorating today. Your teacher is right actually, it won't be done until December 24th. To be precise, just the tree is decorated then. You can set up the lights and other decorations earlier. Most people here start this around December 1st, with the start of Advent, so you can enjoy the glitter for the whole month. And no, I've never been to America, but I've seen the wonderful decorations in movies."

Maria hands each child a box and takes one for herself. On the way up she adds, „I would like to look through everything and then bring a few things to the children's home. They have a lot of new children there and I thought they would be happy if it looked festive during Advent."

After hauling the boxes to the kitchen table, Alessia pulls the closest one over and begins to unfold the lid. Her fingers move slowly as her mind ponders the conversation.

Maria can't help but notice how busily her teenage daughter is working to unpack her thoughts.

„Mom," Alessia begins without looking up, „have you guys ever wanted to break up, Papa and you?"

Surprised by such a question, her mother looks at her and walks over. „No, my dear. We have never wanted that. How did you come up with such an idea?" She strokes the young woman's straight hair and listens attentively.

„Hmm, you know, Dina cried really badly in school today. She told me how her parents always argue and that she is afraid that they will split up. If they do, she doesn't know who she would live with because she likes them both you know? Actually, her dad is hardly at home, but when he's there they seem to argue a lot."

She looks at her reflection in a red Christmas ball and purses her lips.

Alessia's mother puts a hand on her shoulder and sighs: „Yes, that's definitely not nice for Dina. But I am sure that her parents want what is best for her and that they will find a good solution. Maybe Dina would like to come over to think about something else? What do you think about that? She is welcome to join us for dinner and we will accompany her home."

Her daughter's eyes widen and look to her mother in horror. „Here? But then she will see how poor we are. She lives in this white villa up on the hill, Mama! I would be very embarrassed."

„Alessia, there is nothing to be ashamed of here! Even if we don't have as much money as Dina's or others' families, we lack nothing.

And most importantly, we have each other. I am sure Dina will have a lot of fun eating with us. And if I remember correctly, isn't she fond of Bent?" Maria nudges her daughter with her hip and walks around the table with a grin.

„Oh wow, Timon, what kind of artwork have you made out of these things in this short time?" She picks up a lump of glitter and sighs: „Do you think you can untangle that again? I cannot give a gift that looks like this."

She looks questioningly at her creative son and lets the lump dangle back and forth in front of his face.

„Why not? This is a Christmas bomb, Mom! When it goes off, it glitters everywhere! Don't you think the children in the foster home would be happy about a glitter bomb,

Mom?" Full of euphoria and excitement, he picks up his creation and looks at it proudly. Maria shakes her head with a smile and turns to the other things on the table.

„Can I call her right now, Mom? I don't want to ask her in front of everyone at school. That would be weird, because we're not best friends or anything." Alessia looks at her mother questioningly.

„I think that's a good idea, dear. And if her mom wants to talk to me, I'm here to defuse the Christmas bomb." With a smile, Maria sits down at the kitchen table and begins to bring some order to the Christmas decoration chaos.

December 22, 2021

Jonas steps through the heavy snow in front of his house and is surprised by the white Porsche Cayenne in his driveway. He looks carefully at the vehicle as he passes it and whistles appreciatively. He brushes the snow off his boots and plugs in the Christmas lights by the front entrance. After a quick, satisfied look back, he opens the door and enters the warm house.

„Maria, I cannot accept that gift, my dear. I love the car, but maybe it's best if we don't give each other gifts. Then again, beggers can't be choosers!"

His laughter is interrupted by Maria with a waving hand gesture. She walks up to him, takes his coat and whispers; „Dina's mother is here and is crying her heart out. I'm in the kitchen with her, the kids are watching a Christmas movie and I think it would be best if you could join them too. I made two big pizzas so you won't starve to death. Is that okay with you?"

She looks at him questioningly, already knowing his answer.

„Pizza and Christmas movie on a perfectly normal Wednesday? Of course that's ok with me! I hope Dina's mom will be better soon. As always, you are an angel to everyone, Maria." Jonas kisses his wife on the cheek then claps his hands and walks down the steps to the TV room in the basement.

„I hope you haven't eaten all of the pizza!

This cold weather has made Papa really hungry!"

Maria goes back into the dining room and puts another box of Kleenex in front of the sobbing woman. The elegant woman graciously pulls out a tissue with her manicured fingers and continues to sob.

„I feel terrible, Maria! I sit here and cry my misery out to you while the children and husband eat pizza and watch movies in the basement... I'm so sorry, it wasn't my intention to burst in here. But when you asked me how I was doing, it just happened... I don't even know when my husband last had something to eat with Dina and me, let alone watched a movie with her... We don't really do anything as a family these days. He is so busy with his job, there is not much freedom left. And when he has some time, he goes to the golf course to relax because that calms him down, he says... I understand that too. He hardly has any time for himself, but that leaves Dina and me outside... That is no family. I didn't imagine it like this at all, Maria… I don't want it that way anymore." While her loud thoughts come, tears continue to roll down her cheeks and suppressed sobs threaten to explode. She blows her nose noisily and looks sadly at Maria.

„How did you imagine it, Lisa?" Maria sits across from her and folds her hands as if in prayer.

„I don't know really, like you guys, I guess... I wish that he would come home at an appropriate time in the evening, sit down with us at the set table and enjoy his two girls."

Maria smiles lovingly and raises an eyebrow. „Can you cook, Lisa?"

Irritated, the crying woman blinks at Maria and shrugs her shoulders. „I... I can cook certain things... but... well... that was a long time ago..." She swallows forcefully and blows her nose again. „My mom always said that the way to a man's heart is through his stomach... but that's stupid peasant chatter!" As soon as she said it, she regrets her cheeky interpretation and looks at Maria apologetically. „That... I didn't mean it that way, Maria, sorry."

Maria waves it away with a laugh. „Oh, I don't call ourselves farmers just because we have chickens and Jonas is a construction worker. Don't worry, I won't take it personally, but I know that everyone in my family really appreciates having delicious, homemade meals. And I couldn't cook before I was married. But the joy and gratitude that every meal on the faces of my loved ones taught me to try many dishes, even if it's just a sandwich or a homemade pizza." She looks at her weathered hands and rubs them together.

„What are you going to do on Christmas Eve, Lisa?"

Before Lisa can open her mouth, Timon flies into the kitchen with his hands up high in the air.

„Dad told me I should wash my hands! Mom, the pizza is sooooo delicious! I wanted to eat more of it, but dad said I would burst and it would be an ugly mess! Mom, has someone ever burst because they ate too much pizza?" The small, cheerful chatterbox walks to the tap and does as he was told.

„No, Timon, I don't think that has happened before. But I'm glad to hear that you liked the pizza. Was there enough for everyone?"

„I don't know, Dad is the only one eating now, but he said there will be definitely a delicious dessert waiting for us. Is that true, Mom?"

Maria feels the anticipation as not one, but two pairs of eyes wait expectedly for her answer. She glances between Lisa and her son and replies with a grin…

„You guys caught me right there. Papa knows me well. I'll bring the dessert down in a moment, let it be a surprise."

„Hurray! Dessert, dessert!!" Timon walks back towards the basement with clenched fists, confident of victory.

December 23, 2021

All five family members look at the festively decorated dining room with satisfaction. The chain of candlesticks at the window enchants the room with a warm light. Colorful bulbs which hang merrily from the ceiling, dance in the warm candlelight that spreads from the table.

„They should be here any minute, Mom." Excited, Alessia walks to the window and presses her nose against the cold pane. Nothing can be seen in the darkness apart from snow.

„They? Who else is joining us for dinner today besides Dina?" Jonas puts his hands on his hips and looks around. „Why am I always the last to find out about the news in this family?"

„Because you work all day, Papa! And you don't seem to be very attentive. Have you counted the plates on the table? „Alessia laughs and walks towards the kitchen.

„Mama does so too. Well, language lessons on the computer are not exactly the same as my work, but still..." Jonas finishes his fun.

„Hey, you take that back! I earn my own pocket money. Lisa will be joining us for dinner as well. After all, we still have a lot to discuss."

„Oha! That sounds like another Christmas movie with a popcorn fight. But I decide what film we are watching today!" Jonas rubs his hands and is about to go to the rack with the DVDs when the doorbell rings.

„I'll get it!" Alessia scurries out of the kitchen towards the direction of the door and jerks it open.

„Come on in! We have been waiting for a long time." Alessia's happy mood sets the tone for a warm welcome. Dina and her mother enter the warm house and have Jonas take their coats.

„Welcome, ladies," Jonas greets them and steps aside for his wife.

Maria hugs Lisa while Dina goes into the dining room with Alessia.

„It's wonderful to have you here, Lisa. Will Anthony join us later?" Maria smiles gently at these words, without making any assumption.

Lisa shrugs her shoulders and sighs. „If I don't expect it, then I am not disappointed. But who knows, maybe his curiosity is greater than the importance of his network gathering today. Some of his customers meet for a Christmas slumber. He doesn't like to miss these events." She takes a deep breath and walks with Maria into the deliciously smelling dining room.

„You are sitting there and you are here. You there and you there!"

Timon points with his little index finger to the assigned places at the table and everyone follows his instructions without any further comment.

„Good decisions, my young man. That gives this table a new dynamic. I think it's great." Jonas claps his hands and lifts the lid of the hot bowl.

„Off to the land of milk and honey! Hmm... Maria, this stew smells heavenly! I don't think anyone except me will like it. Everything for me!" Jonas laughs mischievously and winks at Dina. „I will share something with you today, Dina, because you are our guest. Hand me your bowl."

Everyone at the table laughs and Dina holds up her bowl with red cheeks.

***

„Maria, the food and the company were wonderful! I would like to thank you all very much for your hospitality. Are you sure that Dina can sleep here? Is that not too much?"

„You are very welcome. Yes, I am sure. The girls have so much fun together. Christmas couldn't be better for the two of them."

Maria takes Lisa's coat off the hook when Jonas joins them.

„Lisa, could you please give me Anthony's phone number?"

Both women look at him in surprise. Jonas puts both hands in his trouser pockets and shrugs his shoulders.

„What then? Can't I have a new friend for myself, too?" Jonas glances at the two of them with a grin and stops his gaze at Lisa, waiting for an answer.

„Um... Yes, of course, I can. Do you have your cell phone here? Or do you want to give me your number, then I'll text it to you." Lisa takes out her iPhone and opens her contacts when Jonas answers;

„Just leave it where it is, that little cheater machine. I like to activate my brain every day by remembering whatever I can. You just have to tell me his number." He taps his forehead with his index finger and winks at her mischievously.

„Oh wow, really? I have to cheat here anyway, because I have no idea what his number is." Caught, she screws up her mouth and starts typing on the screen. She reads the numbers slowly and Jonas nods intently.

„All right, then we'll see you tomorrow. I'm looking forward to a particularly lively Christmas Eve." He extends a strong hand to Lisa and gives her a friendly smile when she says goodbye.

Christmas eve

There is hustle and bustle in the kitchen as different scents meet in the air. The children cut out the Christmas cookies and place one oven tray on top of the other. Maria wraps the large roast in slices of bacon and then into the homemade dough. Christmas music is playing in the background and everyone is busy in their anticipation, humming or moving to the familiar melodies.

„What a great Christmas this is. The festival of love for family and friends!" Jonas spreads his arms as if he wanted to hug the world. Maria accepts this as an invitation and cuddles up to him.

„Hmm, that's nice. Thank you my dear. I will now dare the ultimate call. Wish me luck. There is something about lawyers that takes me out of my comfort zone." The family man gives his wife a loving look.

„You will master it. It's not about the lawyer in him. From papa to papa, from husband to husband." Maria lets herself be kissed on the forehead and goes back to her work of art.

„Mom, why is Dina's dad so different from mine? Doesn't he love his family?" Timon is about to put a piece of dough in his mouth when Alessia takes it from his hand.

„Stop eating the dough, there are worms in it when it's not baked! Surely, he loves Dina and his wife.

But he has a very stressful job and little free time. But that means they can buy and experience all these beautiful things. I mean, did you see, they even have a TV in the car, that's so awesome." Alessia continues to add to her star-shaped cookie cutouts.

„What's the point of it all? Staring at a screen in the white leather armchair, but no dad to cuddle with? No fun family games and no meals together? Let's be honest, Alessia, you can see how money doesn't necessarily make you happy, right?" The oldest of the children collapses on a chair and looks at his almond croissants. „My teacher once said; 'You can buy beautiful things with money, but you can't bring back the missed moments of love'.

„Aww, he said that very nicely, Bent. How right he is. And

now, let's hope that Dad will manage to persuade Dina's father to consider how nice it is to choose and fell your own Christmas tree in the forest." Maria joins the table and admires the great cookies.

She was just about to comment on the works of art when Jonas comes back into the kitchen with a beaming face. He claps his hands and says cheerfully, „Well then, off to the woods! We'll bring the most beautiful tree! It can be a little bigger this year, since two guys are carrying it. I hope you are ready with the nicest decorations!" He points his finger around and Alessia jumps up from the chair.

„That means Dina's father has time and is going with you?!" She hugs her father happily, who pats her gently on the back.

„It didn't even take that much persuasion. I was well prepared. As soon as I mentioned the chainsaw, the deal was made. Apparently, that's something he has always wanted to do.“

„Well then, have fun both of you and take good care of him.“ Maria takes a tray and pushes it into the preheated oven.

***

„I have never seen such a magnificent and beautiful Christmas tree in my entire life. Maria and Jonas, my family and I don't know how we can ever thank you for this wonderful evening.“ Anthony takes his wife's hand as he lifts his glass of champagne, which they brought to the party.

Jonas lifts his beer and nods amicably to him. „I'm glad you didn't want to clear the whole forest out of sheer joy with the chainsaw. And thank you for understanding that I prefer to stick with the beer."

„Cheers to all of us and to an unforgettable Christmas! Let's light the candles on the tree and sing something. Then the children can open their presents, otherwise nobody will sit still at the dining table."

Maria picks up the long box of matches and lights the first candle on the tree. At this very moment, a wonderful song resounds, like the voice of an angel. Everyone looks surprised at the elegant, blonde woman who has closed her eyes, one hand on her flat stomach and in the other a full champagne glass. She shapes her red lips new with every syllable and sings with a hearty and lovely voice.

„Oh Christmas Tree".

As soon as she has let the last note fade away, everyone claps their hands happily and lets their enthusiasm run wild.

„Lisa, that was the most beautiful rendition of „Oh Christmas Tree" that I have ever heard. Where did you learn to sing so beautifully?" Jonas is still shaking his head, fascinated.

Before Lisa can answer him, Anthony pulls her to his side again and looks at her as if enchanted.

„I married the most talented opera singer in all of Warsaw. When I first heard her sing on stage, I knew, that is her! I want to marry that angel." Anthony proudly kisses her forehead. Dina stands nearby, smiling ear-to-ear.

„I studied music and singing, but that was a long time ago. I haven't sung for such a long time. This moment and this contemplative atmosphere just cast a spell over me." Linda is beaming with joy at the company. „But please, can we all sing a song together? I didn't want to grab it just for myself."

„Hm, that's going to be difficult now, because usually I'm the songbird in the family." Everyone bursts out laughing at Jonas' attempt of a joke.

Together they sing all the classic Christmas carols, enjoying the atmosphere in the warm light of the Christmas tree.

One gift after the other is opened and the joyful children's eyes light up the room even more.

Anthony refills his wife's champagne glass and sits down at her side.

„My dear, I know, the last few weeks have been very lonely for you and Dina, months even. I missed you very much, even if I can't always communicate it that way. When Jonas called me today, I was in the middle of a meeting and thought that something had happened to Dina or you. Like scales falling from my eyes, I realized how much I miss the two of you each and every day. I am so grateful that Jonas took me to choose this wonderful fir tree. I'm very sorry, Lisa."

„We missed you very much, as well, Anthony. It's great that we can experience such a Christmas party with new friends. But tell me how did the meeting go? Did you get the new mandate?"

„It went really well! No mandate, but that means more time with my two favorite women!"

He kisses his wife on the cheek and toasts to Jonas and Maria gratefully.

***

***

Merry Christmas to y'all!

Have a merry Christmas 2021 with your families, old and new friends and neighbors.

Thank you very much for your loyalty to my stories.

Your Hiam

**

Hiam Mondini

is a Swiss author from the canton of Zug in Switzerland. Hiam lived in Chicago for three years.

2019,

Hiam started a series of scenes with her first Christmas story **'A Tooth Fairy for Christmas'**, which she observed and experienced herself in everyday life in the USA.

2020

With another Christmas in Chicagoland was just around the corner, Hiam did her best to keep a watchful eye and joyful ideas in the air during the pandemic year with the story **'A sleuth for Christmas'**.

2021

After three years in the USA, Hiam returned to her home canton of Zug, Switzerland, and was introduced to a new home. Intercultural encounters on different levels not only preoccupied her two children, but also herself.

In this Christmas story **'No Mandate for Christmas'** Hiam brings the thoughts of love, wealth, and the true values of life to paper.

***

This beautiful cover was designed by **Angelina Brianna Mondini**, 11 years young.